THE MISTAKE

PALAK

Made with ♥ on the Notion Press Platform
www.notionpress.com

As I opened my eyes , I found myself in hospital. I saw a lady , maybe in her 50s was talking to the doctor. "Why am I here?" I asked as I saw her heading towards me. "Oh finally you got back your consciousness. Wait I'll just call the doctor." She said. She was happy like really happy. After the doctor did a quick check-up of mine , the lady sat beside me. "You were in coma during these five years." She said. I was shocked because it's already been five years and I was here the whole time. "Who shot you?" She asked.

"I'm back", I said as I pushed the door of my house. "Oh you are already here", said my brother , Charles standing on the stairs with a dish full of french fries . He took a piece and dipped it in the ketchup, spilling it on the floor. "No it's my ghost, and can't you just eat properly you pig", I said staring at the ketchup on the floor. He rolled his eyes and went to his room without saying anything. "Can't you just stop calling him pig?" My bestie said as he entered the hall. Darren is my best friend since we were kids. After the death of my parents, his family had helped us a lot . "Its fun to tease him. I just love his reaction every time I call him pig." I said while washing the blood off my hands. He smiled, "so childish. Who can say that the so called mafia queen is actually this childish", he said while adjusting his shirt. "Why did you kill him?" he asked. " Well he dared to challenge my power so I showed him." I said while walking towards him." Go and change food is almost ready", Darren's mom said.

I came to my room , took a shower, got into my pajamas and threw myself on my bed looking at the celling replaying my whole day and every single scene when I killed that jerk. I killed him because he was creating problems in my business.

"Mia , you done? Dinner is placed on the dining table .", Darren asked as he knocked on the door. I went downstairs for dinner with him. "Aunty I am thinking about taking a break", I said while putting a spoon full of fried rice in my mouth." "It's a good idea. So when does your break starts?" she asked. "As soon as I'll deal with those morons", I answered. Yes I am talking about the Christopher family . The one who killed my parents. I was 12 when they broke out in our house and killed my parents and Darren's father. Charles was just 9 when it happened. Till this day I'm keeping him safe from those killers. I won't let anyone to cause any harm to him.

One of our gang members came running and screaming my name. "What's wrong ?" I asked. "Mam we found an injured guy in the car. He is covered in blood", he said while taking deep breath. "Bring him in right now ." I said panicking. They brought him in. I ordered them to place him in the guest room and call the doctor. I looked at him , his white shirt soaked in blood , face and hands covered in blood.

Doctor arrived , "please wait outside" the doctor said. We went outside the door , as I was eager to know what happened with him . "He is fine now. You can meet him." The doctor said. I went to the room and saw him on the bed with the blanket that was covering his body as he wasn't wearing the shirt now because of bandages. "He look pale", I thought . I sat on the couch with my one leg placed on the other. "Who are you", I asked. "Keven", he answered.

" Wher...." As I was about to ask where he came from aunt interrupted. "He just got his consciousness, stop asking him questions", aunt said. She sent me to my room . I was not able to sleep the whole night as I kept on wondering about the guy, Keven. The next morning I woke up by the sound of my alarm and got downstairs and saw my aunt making pottage. "Are you making food for that guy", I asked. "Yes he is really weak , he needs care and proper food." Aunt replied. I asked her if I can go and feed Keven , well my real motive to do so were the questions I wanted to ask him. Aunt agreed and gave the tray with the bowl of pottage and a glass of water .

I went to the room he was kept in and placed the tray on the bedside table. Keven was awake, he got up as soon as he saw me and sat on the bed. I gave him the pottage and sat on the couch. "Thank you for helping me", he said while blowing the pottage. " Never mind. So where are you from??" I asked. I'm from Kazan. I came here for better job opportunities and got caught by those men." He answered.

"Where is your family?" I asked. "I'm an orphan." He said. I felt bad for him . After he finished eating I took the empty dishes to the kitchen. He asked me about what I do. "You will get to know" I answered.

As Keven was sleeping peacefully, a sound interrupted his sleep . It was the sound of gunshot. Keven headed towards the living area and hid behind the staircase and saw Mia with a gun in her hand and two heavily built men dragging a dead body. There was blood on the floor. A maid came and wiped the blood and soon the floor was as clean as before. No one can say that someone died there and there was blood on it.

Mia's pov:

I was so upset of this bullshit and that jerk so I shoot him and asked my bodyguards to take care of his body. My maid came and wiped the blood and made the floor look flawless. Not more than a minute after I felt someone was hiding behind the staircase and no sooner saw Keven.

"Who are you?" he asked me. Well "I'm the mafia queen and since now you know me , you are not allowed to leave this place anymore." I said.

I know that he is already terrified but I can't afford to take any risk because of him and he is not even in the condition to leave. Yes I'm a Mafia and killing people is the part of my job but I also have a heart and I can't do this to a patient. It's against my morals. I don't understand why people think that we mafias are heartless. I don't know about others but at least I'm not like that.

"I'm not gonna live here even for a single second." He said while panicking. "Oh well then," I said as I grabbed his wrist and started dragging him towards his room. I pushed him on the bed and closed the door from outside to prevent him from escaping. "How could you do this to me? Open the door please, please open the door" he started knocking on the door and screaming. Aunt came to me because of his screams and asked me to explain. I told her everything and asked her not to open the door without my permission. Saying this , I headed towards my room. "I don't think I'll be able to go on a vacation." I said to myself looking at the Eiffel tower on my phone's lock screen. Since I was a kid I always wanted to visit Paris and now that I finally planned for it , all this happened. I stomped in anger.

I went to the bathroom. I added some lavender flavored sea salt to the hot water in the tub , removed my bathrobe and got into the bathing tub full of hot water. I submerged my body into the soothing hot water and let my hands and feet to freely float in the water. "It's so relaxing" I thought to myself. All my stress and anger melted in that water.

Killing and threatening people, smuggling and all these stuff are illegal , I know but I am doing all this because this is what my dad use to do and the main reason are those killers that killed my family. As I was having a relaxing time for myself I heard Darren calling my name. I heard his footsteps heading towards my bathroom , I heard a knock . "Are you in?" Darren asked. "Hmm" I said and heard his footsteps getting down the stairs.

I'm so exhausted because of all these. I really need a vacation. I wish I could. After the bath I got ready for a meeting. Finally after three hours I came back during the midnight. As I was heading towards the stairs , I heard someone crying . The sound was coming from Keven's room. As I walked inside the room , I saw Keven sitting in a corner and weeping. It made me feel bad but I can't help him. I went near him and sat beside him. "You ok?" I asked. "No I'm not" he replied. "I know I shouldn't have done this to you but I also have my reasons to do all these stuff. Yes I'm a Mafia , not because I wanted to but because I have to. I'm mafia because my dad was one and I cant forgive those who killed him. I will kill them one day for sure." I said. We were having a conversation and Keven went to sleep in the middle of the conversation. He looked so beautiful with the light of the moon falling through the window on his face. I don't know when I went to sleep while admiring his beautiful features.

I woke up by the sunlight falling on my eyes and found myself sitting beside Keven. Without disturbing him I went to my room. After the shower I headed downstairs. "When did you come last night?" aunt asked. "During the midnight" I replied. "Should I just call Keven for breakfast or send his food to his room?" She asked me. "Do whatever you want to" I replied. I noticed Keven heading towards the dining table. "If you don't mind can I have breakfast with you all?" Keven asked. Aunt agreed and served him food. After the breakfast I decided to take everyone on a short trip. We went to the trip . Keven looked relaxed and happy and this made me happy.

A few days passed and during this time Keven got really close to us. He became comfortable and is like family now. One night as I was passing through the terrace, I saw Keven sitting on the floor and was looking at the night sky. I went towards him and sat beside him. "It's beautiful isn't it?" I said. "Oh! When did you come?" he exclaimed. "When you were staring at the stars." I said. I asked him what he was doing here at this time. He said that he was unable to sleep so he came here. We started talking and didn't even realized when the night passed. "Look there" Keven told me while pointing towards the sun rise. It's been a long time since I saw this beautiful scenery. The sky looked like someone had scrambled red chalk on the black slate. The smell of wet soil from the last night and the sound of birds added more beauty this morning.

Later me and Keven went to our rooms. I wondered why time passes so quickly every time I am with Keven . Being honest , I feel safe and at peace whenever I'm with him. I am confused about what I feel for him but I like this confusion. As I went down for breakfast, Charles stopped me . "What is it piggy?" I said in a teasing tone. "Don't tell me you didn't remember?" he said. "Is something special today?" I asked. "Come-on today's Darren's birthday you stupid", he said being frustrated. "Oh shit! How can I forget it? What should I do now?" I panicked. I went to Darren and gave him a hug and wished him. I asked Charles about tonight's party for Darren. "I'll be there on time.". I said while leaving for a meeting.

"Finally a party and I'm gonna make it special for Darren" I thought to myself. As soon as I got home I went to my room to change my clothes.

"Hi sweetie, never seen you here" some girls from the party said this to Keven. "Oh hi . Umm I need to go" Keven said. "Where darling?" they asked. "To me of course" I said while getting close to them. Keven stood beside me and held my hand. I knew that he was awkward so I took him to the other side . The party went well. After the party , I thought I ate so much so I decided to go the kitchen to get something to digest this food . As I was passing through the hallway, I heard Keven talking to someone on the phone. "Don't worry they don't know anything about it and I'll make sure they won't ." Keven said on to the person on the call. I went back to my room. "Is he an enemy or maybe a spy ...?" I thought. "But how can he, like everyone loves him so much , how can he break their trust like this. No , Mia you are just thinking too much. But he said he don't have anyone so who was on the call?" all these thoughts kept on flooding my mind preventing me from sleeping.

Next morning when I was heading downstairs I saw Keven and aunt talking and laughing together. "Good Moring" he said. "I heard you last night" I said while having breakfast. "Oh really! But I slept early last night." He said. I noticed his hands were shacking and he was sweating while answering. "I need to something. I can't let him do any harm to my family." I said to myself. " Well I was planning to take all of you on a trip to Paris. Will it be ok?" I asked. "More than ok" Charles replied. "If everyone is ok with that then I'll book the tickets today itself." I said.

After a week later, it's finally the time to go to Paris. Well I'm more excited to go to Paris than anyone else. "There is a reservation for Charles." I said to the receptionist. "Just give me a minute mam. Yes it's a five room reservation. Here are your keys." She replied. " I said. "Ok so we will go for the dinner in a famous restaurant here at 6 o' clock in the evening." I said. The whole day I just slept. In the evening a car came for us and we got in it. We went to the famous restaurant of Paris , from there we were able to see Elfie tower. Charles and Keven ordered some latte and authentic French cuisine whereas I ordered some pizza with extra cheese and hot chocolate, aunt and Keven ordered pasta.

After dinner we went back to our hotel and went to sleep. We spent 2 days visiting all the famous places and monuments and trying French food .

It's the third and the last day of our Paris trip. We planned to visit Eifel tower as it was already night , the tour guide suggested us to visit a night club as the entry was free today. Keven asked me to stay back with him , so I told everyone to go and we will join them later. Everyone left , me and Keven were alone , it was a cloudy winter night, Keven kneeled down and pulled out a box from his overcoat , but that time I just knew that he is my enemy and I threw the box and it fell a little far from us , near a tree . Tears filled my eyes turning them red, my blood started boiling and started rushing in my veins , "I gave you food, my family gave you love and care and you, you betrayed us. You are the worst person I have ever known. I feel so stupid to fall for you , I wanted to spend my whole life with you. But you , you broke all my dreams and you know what I hate you now. I HATE YOU." My voice echoed.

Without thinking about anything I pulled out my gun and pointed it towards him , he wasn't afraid , didn't even flinched , instead he went near the tree and picked up the box and came to me," I don't know what are you talking about and I would never even think about betraying you and your family. I love you and that's why I got this ring to propose you. That day when you said that you heard me , I was scared that my surprise won't remain a surprise anymore. But when you didn't said anything ,I felt relaxed. I don't know what you thought or what are you talking about but I know one thing for sure I never thought bad about you or this family. I just love you , I wanna marry you , wanna have a small happy family with you and that's all I know." He said with tears in his eyes . I immediately knew that he wasn't lying . I put my gun down and suddenly I felt something penetrated my arm , because of the force I fell off the cliff . I saw someone shooting Keven also and with the sound of the gunshot I felt my head bumped on the floor and all my memories playing in front of me like a movie . I saw my parents hugging me and then everything went black and a tear fell from my lifeless eye.

"The mistake of mine took it's prize,

And without knowing who it was

I won't leave this life ."

Palak is a fantasy author who lives in a world of magic and adventure. She loves to write stories that are suitable for certain age groups, and she loves to connect with her readers through her work . Palak has published few novellas, and she's working on a new series that will take readers on an epic adventure.

She believes that dream can be your reality if one dares to take the risk and if someone can see something in their head , they can touch it with their hand.

Contents

Prologue

As I opened my eyes , I found myself in hospital. I saw a lady , maybe in her 50s was talking to the doctor. “Why am I here?” I asked as I saw her heading towards me. “Oh finally you got back your consciousness. Wait I’ll just call the doctor.” She said. She was happy like really happy. After the doctor did a quick check-up of mine , the lady sat beside me. “You were in coma during these five years.” She said. I was shocked because it’s already been five years and I was here the whole time. “Who shot you?” She asked.

“I’m back”, I said as I pushed the door of my house. “Oh you are already here”, said my brother , Charles standing on the stairs with a dish full of french fries . He took a piece and dipped it in the ketchup, spilling it on the floor. “No it’s my ghost, and can’t you just eat properly you pig”, I said staring at the ketchup on the floor. He rolled his eyes and went to his room without saying anything. “Can’t you just stop calling him pig?” My bestie said as he entered the hall. Darren is my best friend since we were kids. After the death of my parents, his family had helped us a lot . “Its fun to tease him. I just love his reaction every time I call him pig.” I said while washing the blood off my hands. He smiled, “so childish. Who can say that the so called mafia queen is actually this childish”, he said while adjusting his shirt. “Why did you kill him?” he asked. “ Well he dared to challenge my power so I showed him.” I said while walking towards him.“ Go and change food is almost ready”, Darren’s mom said.

I came to my room , took a shower, got into my pajamas and threw myself on my bed looking at the celling replaying my whole day and every single scene when I killed that jerk. I killed him because he was creating problems in my business.

“Mia , you done? Dinner is placed on the dining table .”, Darren asked as he knocked on the door. I went downstairs for dinner with him. “Aunty I am thinking about taking a break”, I said while putting a spoon full of fried rice in my mouth.” “It’s a good idea. So when does your break starts?” she asked. “As soon as I’ll deal with those morons”, I answered. Yes I am talking about the Christopher family . The one who killed my parents. I was 12 when they broke out in our house and killed my parents and Darren’s father. Charles was just 9 when it happened. Till this day I’m keeping him safe from those killers. I won’t let anyone to cause any harm to him.

One of our gang members came running and screaming my name. “What’s wrong ?” I asked. “Mam we found an injured guy in the car. He is covered in blood”, he said while taking deep breath. “Bring him in right now .” I said panicking. They brought him in. I ordered them to place him in the guest room and call the doctor. I looked at him , his white shirt soaked in blood , face and hands covered in blood.

Doctor arrived , “please wait outside” the doctor said. We went outside the door , as I was eager to know what happened with him . “He is fine now. You can meet him.” The doctor said. I went to the room and saw him on the bed with the blanket that was covering his body as he wasn’t wearing the shirt now because of bandages. “He look pale”, I thought . I sat on the couch with my one leg placed on the other. “Who are you”, I asked. “Keven”, he answered.

“ Wher....” As I was about to ask where he came from aunt interrupted. “He just got his consciousness, stop asking him questions”, aunt said. She sent me to my room

. I was not able to sleep the whole night as I kept on wondering about the guy, Keven. The next morning I woke up by the sound of my alarm and got downstairs and saw my aunt making pottage. “Are you making food for that guy”, I asked. “Yes he is really weak , he needs care and proper food.” Aunt replied. I asked her if I can go and feed Keven , well my real motive to do so were the questions I wanted to ask him. Aunt agreed and gave the tray with the bowl of pottage and a glass of water .

I went to the room he was kept in and placed the tray on the bedside table. Keven was awake, he got up as soon as he saw me and sat on the bed. I gave him the pottage and sat on the couch. “Thank you for helping me”, he said while blowing the pottage. “ Never mind. So where are you from??” I asked. I’m from Kazan. I came here for better job opportunities and got caught by those men.” He answered.

“Where is your family?” I asked. “I’m an orphan.” He said. I felt bad for him . After he finished eating I took the empty dishes to the kitchen. He asked me about what I do. “You will get to know” I answered.

As Keven was sleeping peacefully, a sound interrupted his sleep . It was the sound of gunshot. Keven headed towards the living area and hid behind the staircase and saw Mia with a gun in her hand and two heavily built men dragging a dead body. There was blood on the floor. A maid came and wiped the blood and soon the floor was as clean as before. No one can say that someone died there and there was blood on it.

Mia’s pov:

I was so upset of this bullshit and that jerk so I shoot him and asked my bodyguards to take care of his body. My maid came and wiped the blood and made the floor look flawless. Not more than a minute after I felt someone was hiding behind the staircase and no sooner saw Keven.

"Who are you?" he asked me. Well "I'm the mafia queen and since now you know me , you are not allowed to leave this place anymore." I said.

I know that he is already terrified but I can't afford to take any risk because of him and he is not even in the condition to leave. Yes I'm a Mafia and killing people is the part of my job but I also have a heart and I can't do this to a patient. It's against my morals. I don't understand why people think that we mafias are heartless. I don't know about others but at least I'm not like that.

"I'm not gonna live here even for a single second." He said while panicking. "Oh well then," I said as I grabbed his wrist and started dragging him towards his room. I pushed him on the bed and closed the door from outside to prevent him from escaping. "How could you do this to me? Open the door please, please open the door" he started knocking on the door and screaming. Aunt came to me because of his screams and asked me to explain. I told her everything and asked her not to open the door without my permission. Saying this , I headed towards my room. "I don't think I'll be able to go on a vacation." I said to myself looking at the Eiffel tower on my phone's lock screen. Since I was a kid I always wanted to visit Paris and now that I finally planned for it , all this happened. I stomped in anger.

I went to the bathroom. I added some lavender flavored sea salt to the hot water in the tub , removed my bathrobe and got into the bathing tub full of hot water. I submerged my body into the soothing hot water and let my hands and feet to freely float in the water. "It's so relaxing" I thought to myself. All my stress and anger melted in that water.

Killing and threatening people, smuggling and all these stuff are illegal , I know but I am doing all this because this is what my dad use to do and the main reason are those killers that killed my family. As I was having a relaxing time for myself I heard Darren calling my name. I heard his footsteps heading towards my bathroom , I heard a knock . "Are you in?" Darren asked. "Hmm" I said and heard his footsteps getting down the stairs.

I'm so exhausted because of all these. I really need a vacation. I wish I could. After the bath I got ready for a meeting. Finally after three hours I came back during the midnight. As I was heading towards the stairs , I heard someone crying . The sound was coming from Keven's room. As I walked inside the room , I saw Keven sitting in a corner and weeping. It made me feel bad but I can't help him. I went near him and sat beside him. "You ok?" I asked. "No I'm not" he replied. "I know I shouldn't have done this to you but I also have my reasons to do all these stuff. Yes I'm a Mafia , not because I wanted to but because I have to. I'm mafia because my dad was one and I cant forgive those who killed him. I will kill them one day for sure." I said. We were having a conversation and Keven went to sleep in the middle of the conversation. He looked so beautiful with the light of the moon falling through the window on his face. I don't know when I went to sleep while admiring his beautiful features.

I woke up by the sunlight falling on my eyes and found myself sitting beside Keven. Without disturbing him I went to my room. After the shower I headed downstairs. "When did you come last night?" aunt asked. "During the midnight" I replied. "Should I just call Keven for breakfast or send his food to his room?" She asked me. "Do whatever you want to" I replied. I noticed Keven heading towards the dining table. "If you don't mind can I have breakfast with you all?" Keven asked. Aunt agreed and served him food.

After the breakfast I decided to take everyone on a short trip. We went to the trip . Keven looked relaxed and happy and this made me happy.

A few days passed and during this time Keven got really close to us. He became comfortable and is like family now. One night as I was passing through the terrace, I saw Keven sitting on the floor and was looking at the night sky. I went towards him and sat beside him. "It's beautiful isn't it?" I said. "Oh! When did you come?" he exclaimed. "When you were staring at the stars." I said. I asked him what he was doing here at this time. He said that he was unable to sleep so he came here. We started talking and didn't even realized when the night passed. "Look there" Keven told me while pointing towards the sun rise. It's been a long time since I saw this beautiful scenery. The sky looked like someone had scrambled red chalk on the black slate. The smell of wet soil from the last night and the sound of birds added more beauty this morning.

Later me and Keven went to our rooms. I wondered why time passes so quickly every time I am with Keven . Being honest , I feel safe and at peace whenever I'm with him. I am confused about what I feel for him but I like this confusion. As I went down for breakfast, Charles stopped me . "What is it piggy?" I said in a teasing tone. "Don't tell me you didn't remember?" he said. "Is something special today?" I asked. "Come-on today's Darren's birthday you stupid", he said being frustrated. "Oh shit! How can I forget it? What should I do now?" I panicked. I went to Darren and gave him a hug and wished him. I asked Charles about tonight's party for Darren. "I'll be there on time.". I said while leaving for a meeting.

"Finally a party and I'm gonna make it special for Darren" I thought to myself. As soon as I got home I went to my room to change my clothes.

"Hi sweetie, never seen you here" some girls from the party said this to Keven. "Oh hi . Umm I need to go" Keven said. "Where darling?" they asked. "To me of course" I said while getting close to them. Keven stood beside me and held my hand. I knew that he was awkward so I took him to the other side . The party went well. After the party , I thought I ate so much so I decided to go the kitchen to get something to digest this food . As I was passing through the hallway, I heard Keven talking to someone on the phone. "Don't worry they don't know anything about it and I'll make sure they won't ." Keven said on to the person on the call. I went back to my room. "Is he an enemy or maybe a spy ...?" I thought. "But how can he, like everyone loves him so much , how can he break their trust like this. No , Mia you are just thinking too much. But he said he don't have anyone so who was on the call?" all these thoughts kept on flooding my mind preventing me from sleeping.

Next morning when I was heading downstairs I saw Keven and aunt talking and laughing together. "Good Moring" he said. "I heard you last night" I said while having breakfast. "Oh really! But I slept early last night." He said. I noticed his hands were shacking and he was sweating while answering. "I need to something. I can't let him do any harm to my family." I said to myself. " Well I was planning to take all of you on a trip to Paris. Will it be ok?" I asked. "More than ok" Charles replied. "If everyone is ok with that then I'll book the tickets today itself." I said.

After a week later, it's finally the time to go to Paris. Well I'm more excited to go to Paris than anyone else. "There is a reservation for Charles." I said to the receptionist. "Just give me a minute mam. Yes it's a five room reservation. Here are your keys." She replied. " I said.

“Ok so we will go for the dinner in a famous restaurant here at 6 o’ clock in the evening.” I said. The whole day I just slept. In the evening a car came for us and we got in it. We went to the famous restaurant of Paris , from there we were able to see Elfie tower. Charles and Keven ordered some latte and authentic French cuisine whereas I ordered some pizza with extra cheese and hot chocolate, aunt and Keven ordered pasta.

After dinner we went back to our hotel and went to sleep. We spent 2 days visiting all the famous places and monuments and trying French food .

It’s the third and the last day of our Paris trip. We planned to visit Eifel tower as it was already night , the tour guide suggested us to visit a night club as the entry was free today. Keven asked me to stay back with him , so I told everyone to go and we will join them later. Everyone left , me and Keven were alone , it was a cloudy winter night, Keven kneeled down and pulled out a box from his overcoat , but that time I just knew that he is my enemy and I threw the box and it fell a little far from us , near a tree . Tears filled my eyes turning them red, my blood started boiling and started rushing in my veins , “I gave you food, my family gave you love and care and you, you betrayed us. You are the worst person I have ever known. I feel so stupid to fall for you , I wanted to spend my whole life with you. But you , you broke all my dreams and you know what I hate you now. I HATE YOU.” My voice echoed.

Without thinking about anything I pulled out my gun and pointed it towards him , he wasn’t afraid , didn’t even flinched , instead he went near the tree and picked up the box and came to me,” I don’t know what are you talking about and I would never even think about betraying you and your family. I love you and that’s why I got this ring to propose you. That day when you said that you heard me , I was scared that my surprise won't remain a surprise anymore. But when you didn't said anything ,I felt relaxed. I don't know what you thought or what are you talking about but I know one thing for sure I never thought bad about you or this family. I just love you , I wanna marry you , wanna have a small happy family with you and that's all I know." He said with tears in his eyes . I immediately knew that he wasn't lying . I put my gun down and suddenly I felt something penetrated my arm , because of the force I fell off the cliff . I saw someone shooting Keven also and with the sound of the gunshot I felt my head bumped on the floor and all my memories playing in front of me like a movie . I saw my parents hugging me and then everything went black and a tear fell from my lifeless eye.

"The mistake of mine took it's prize,
And without knowing who it was
I won't leave this life ."

Palak is a fantasy author who lives in a world of magic and adventure. She loves to write stories that are suitable for certain age groups, and she loves to connect with her readers through her work . Palak has published few novellas, and she's working on a new series that will take readers on an epic adventure.

She believes that dream can be your reality if one dares to take the risk and if someone can see something in their head , they can touch it with their hand.

Printed by Libri Plureos GmbH in Hamburg,
Germany